BJ DOG

By Stan Cullimore

Illustrated by Karen Hayles

Fife Council Education Department
King's Road Primary School
King's Crescent, Rosyth KY11 2RS

Chapter 1
BJ Arrives

Johnny Buckett sat down at the breakfast table and looked sleepily at the empty cereal bowl in front of him.

He yawned, and pulled the blue dressing gown tighter round his shoulders.

"Brr," he shivered. "It's freezing." He put down the spoon he was holding, placed his bare feet on the floor and reached for the pack of Cornflakes he had just taken out of the cupboard.

He picked it up and shook it.

"Rats," he grumbled. "They're almost finished." He hated all the powdery stuff at the bottom. But he always ate it, he had to, his Mum made him. She said it was full of vitamins.

Slowly a grin spread itself across Johnny's face.

"Mum's not here today," he thought. "So I can throw it all in the bin and open a new pack. Great!"

He frowned. Something was wrong. What was it? He put down the packet of cornflakes, and stared at the half empty bottle of milk on the table.

Suddenly it dawned on him – the floor was freezing.

"Yikes," he yelped. "My feet! They're frozen solid. Argh…"

Without thinking, he threw himself back in his chair, and yanked both his feet off the ground.

It was not a good thing to do. The chair tipped back, and started to slide slowly along the floor.

"Uh-oh," Johnny hooked both his feet under the table and gulped. All of a sudden, he felt wide awake. He leant forward slightly, and the chair wobbled.

"OK," he said to himself slowly. "How do I get out of this?" He noticed that the table had started to lift off the ground where his feet were touching it.

He didn't have much time.

"If I move, I'm going to end up lying on the coldest floor in the world, covered in milk and powdery cornflakes."

The chair groaned beneath him.

"And if I don't move, I'm going to end up lying on the coldest floor in the world, covered in milk and powdery cornflakes. It's a no-win situation."

He gulped. It was time to do something drastic.

"Help," he squeaked, closing his eyes and wishing he was back in his nice warm bed.

There was a noise from outside the breakfast room window, as if someone was clearing their throat.

"I say," said a muffled voice through the glass, "what are you doing?"

"Is that you Dad?" asked Johnny hopefully.

"No," replied the voice.

"Then who is it?"

"It's me, BJ," replied the voice. "How do you do?"

"Huh! Who's BJ?" Johnny opened his eyes and looked.

"Oh!" He closed his eyes, and then opened them again, slowly. He wanted to make sure that they weren't playing tricks on him.

But they had been right the first time.

There, smiling at him through the breakfast room window, was a perfectly normal Scottie dog. Except for one thing – it was wearing a monocle!

"I must be dreaming," thought Johnny. He looked closely at the dog and smiled as if he felt a bit foolish. Which he did. "For a minute there, I thought you could talk."

The dog nodded happily. "You were right. I can!"

"Argh!" For the second time that morning, Johnny

threw himself backwards in his chair. There was a loud crash, followed by a low groan. As he lay on the coldest floor in the world, covered in milk and powdery cornflakes, Johnny sighed. "That was definitely not a Good Thing to Do."

"Then why did you do it," asked BJ. "Hmm?"

Five minutes later, Johnny tiptoed quietly into his mum and dad's bedroom carrying a tray.

"Dad, are you awake?" he whispered.

His father coughed noisily, then rolled over and grunted. "No."

"Do you want a cup of tea?"

His father opened one eye suspiciously. "What did you say?" he croaked.

"I said – do you want a cup of tea. Only I've made you one." Johnny set the tray down on his father's bedside cabinet and lifted up a mug of steaming tea. "Here you are, Dad. Sit up."

For a moment nothing happened. Then, slowly, and with a great deal of groaning. His father sat up and took the mug in both hands.

He coughed again. "Thanks Johnny." He took a sip of tea. "By the way, I'm really ill – in case you hadn't already noticed."

Johnny nodded. "Sounds like you've got a cold to me."

"That's what I said."

"You shouldn't have gone out on your bike last night – not in all that rain. You know what Mum will say don't you?"

His father nodded miserably. "She'll say it's my own fault." Suddenly he looked worried. "What time is it Johnny? I haven't got my glasses on."

Johnny looked at the clock. "It's all right Dad. Mum isn't due back from Auntie's for at least fifty-five minutes."

His father sighed and leant back into his pillows.

"Good. That means I can relax. The only thing I've got to do is to wash up the dishes from last night."

"It's all right Dad, I'll do them," Johnny smiled sweetly at his father, and wondered if he was over-doing the creeping.

He was.

His father looked puzzled. "Why are you being so helpful, Johnny?" He glanced at the half-drunk mug of tea in his hand. "You hardly ever bring me tea in bed. And you never offer to do the washing up. What are you after?"

Johnny shrugged. "I'm not after anything." His father snorted. "Well, nothing much, Dad – honest. It's just that there's a dog in the garden, and I was wondering if we could keep it. That's all."

"But I hate dogs!"

"Don't I know it," sighed Johnny – his Dad had 'a thing' about dogs. He was always going on about how much he loathed them.

"But this is no ordinary dog, Dad. Honest!"

His father snorted. "All dogs are ordinary. They all smell, they all poo everywhere and they're all stupid."

Johnny smiled hopefully. "This dog isn't stupid. It's called BJ, and it can talk."

His father put down the empty mug he was holding, and pulled the duvet up to his shoulders.

"Oh, can it? That's useful. In that case, you can tell it to get out of our garden before Mum comes home. She's just planted a whole load of bulbs. And if that dog of yours scratches them up – she'll have his guts for garters. Thanks for the tea, Johnny, it was lovely. Now leave me alone, I'm going back to sleep."

Johnny sighed as he closed the bedroom door behind him. "That's the trouble with parents. They never believe anything you tell them!"

He went down the stairs and squeezed past his father's new mountain bike.

Then he stepped over the puddles of oil and mud that had dripped on to the hallway carpet from the dirty wheels.

"Mum won't be very pleased," he thought. "She doesn't usually let Dad bring his bike into the house." He sighed.

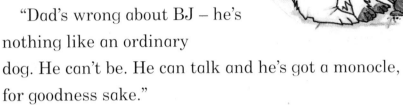

"Dad's wrong about BJ – he's nothing like an ordinary dog. He can't be. He can talk and he's got a monocle, for goodness sake."

He walked into the breakfast room and looked out of the window. "Oh no, I don't believe it!" He closed his eyes, counted to ten, and opened them again. "There again," he sighed, "perhaps he is just like an ordinary dog, after all."

BJ was sitting on the patio, wagging his tail. In his mouth, was one of Mum's newly planted daffodil bulbs.

Two minutes and forty-five seconds later, Johnny was back in his father's bedroom.

"Er, Dad. Do you happen to know where the back door keys are?" He asked casually.

"Ah ... atishoo!" There was a loud sneeze, and Dad's head appeared from under the duvet. "Oh, I'm in a terrible state," he groaned.

"I know, you've already told me once. Do you know where the keys are?" asked Johnny – for the second time. "Only I can't find them anywhere."

"What keys?" His father wrinkled his nose. "Can you pass me a tissue, Johnny?"

Johnny passed him the box of man size tissues. "The back door keys."

His father blew his nose – loudly, and then nodded. "I took them with me last night, when I went out on my bike. I put them back in the cupboard when I came in the back door."

Johnny frowned. "But you didn't come in the back door, Dad. I let you in the front. Remember?"

His father stopped, and thought for a moment. "Yes, you're right. You did." He nodded his head thoughtfully.

Suddenly, he gasped. "My bike," he cried. "Where's my bike? I left it outside. It'll get stolen."

"Relax, Dad," said Johnny. "It's in the hall."

His father sighed. "Thank goodness."

Suddenly, he sat bolt upright in bed, and squawked.

"Relax!" he shouted. "What do you mean relax? If Mum finds it there, she'll kill me." He grabbed his glasses, shoved them on the end of his nose and peered at the bedside clock.

He jumped out of bed, and staggered across to the wardrobe. "Do you realise Johnny, we've only got thirty-five minutes to get my bike out of the house and wash up, before Mum gets home?"

He pulled on a clean pair of boxer shorts and started to get dressed, still chuntering to himself. "It's not fair, I'm ill! I shouldn't be running around like this. Still, I've got to move that bike. I only hope it hasn't made the carpet dirty." He looked up. "Have you got rid of that dog yet?"

Johnny gulped. "Well, er, yes and no, really."

"What do you mean, 'yes and no'?" asked his father, tying up his shoelace.

"Well, what I mean is. Yes, your bike has got the carpet dirty – and no, I haven't got rid of the dog yet."

A few minutes later, Johnny and his father were both standing in the breakfast room – looking worried.

"The way I see it, is this," said Dad. "We have," he glanced up at the kitchen clock, "approximately twenty-nine minutes before your mother arrives home from Auntie Mary's."

Johnny nodded.

"In that time," continued his father, "we have to do the following – one, get my bike out of the house and back into the bike shed. Two, finish the washing up. Three, clean up the mess on the carpet in the hallway. Four, find the back door keys. And five, get that stupid dog out of the garden."

He frowned. "Is there anything I've forgotten?"

"Yes," said Johnny.

"What?"

"We've got to plant all the bulbs that BJ has just dug up."

His father groaned. "What?"

Johnny nodded. "It's not his fault though, he's a dog, that's what they do. You said so yourself."

"We'll never do it, Johnny. We're done for. Mum is going to kill us."

There was a noise from outside the breakfast room window, as if someone was clearing their throat.

"I say," said a muffled voice through the glass. "Is there anything I can do to help?"

"Who said that?" asked Dad.

"Me," replied BJ.

Dad looked out of the window. Two seconds later there was a crash, as Dad fainted and fell to the floor.

"Dad! Are you all right, Dad?" Johnny waved his hand slowly in front of his father's face – there was no reaction. His father looked as if he had just seen a ghost.

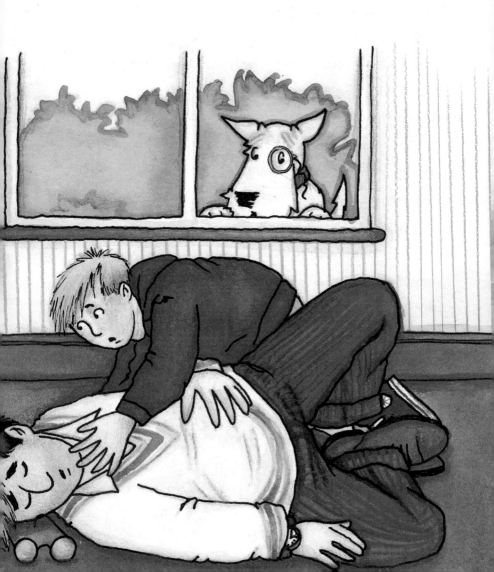

"Is that your father?" asked BJ.

Johnny nodded.

"He looks as if he's just seen a ghost," said BJ.

"Johnny," hissed Dad, gripping him by the elbow. "Am I going mad, or can that dog talk?"

Johnny turned and patted his father on the shoulder.

"Relax, Dad. You're not going any madder than usual. This is BJ, the talking dog I told you about earlier. Let me introduce you. BJ – this is Dad. Dad, this is BJ."

Dad looked at Johnny, as if he was hoping it was all a peculiar joke.

"Hello, Dad," said BJ.

Dad sat up and stared at the small dog that was sitting outside the breakfast room window. Then, he noticed the monocle. He shook his head.

"I'm not dreaming all this am I, Johnny?"

"No," said Johnny.

"Hello BJ," said Dad weakly. "Pleased to meet you, I'm sure."

BJ wagged his tail. "I say," he said. "You'll never guess what I've just found. Look!" He turned round and picked up something that was lying on the ground next to a pile of recently-dug-up daffodil bulbs.

It was a keyring, with several small keys on it.

"I tried to chew it, but it tastes awful."

Johnny whistled. "You know what that is don't you, Dad?"

His father sneezed, and then nodded weakly. "It's the back door keys."

"And you know what that means, don't you?"

"Yes, I do. It means that I must have dropped them in the garden on my way out yesterday."

"And," said Johnny happily. "It also means that BJ is a Hero! He found them – well done BJ."

"I don't think Mum will say that when she sees her daffodil bulbs," muttered Dad.

But Johnny didn't hear him. He had already shot out of the front door, and was racing round to the back of the house, to get the keys off BJ.

Three and a half minutes later, after the bike had been returned to its rightful place in the bike shed, Johnny, his father, and BJ were standing in the hallway staring at the mess on the carpet. It looked terrible.

There were muddy tyre marks leading from the front door to where the bike had leant against the radiator ... and two large puddles of oily water, where the wheels had dripped themselves dry.

"You know what I think?" said Dad.

"No," replied Johnny.

"I think it looks terrible!"

"He's right you know," said BJ. "It does. It looks absolutely awful. Hideous. Ghastly, almost. Atrocious. It makes me feel ill just to look at it."

Dad glared at BJ. "Thank you, BJ. We get the message, now please can you be quiet and let me think."

He thought for a moment. Then, he strode in to the front room to find out what time it was. He came out again, looking more than a little worried.

"Johnny," he said. "We have eighteen and a quarter minutes before your mother gets back. Have you done the washing up yet?"

Johnny shook his head. "Not yet, Dad."

"OK. Off you go and do it then. I'll go into the garden. I've got to re-plant all those daffodil bulbs that A Certain Dog has just dug up."

He glared at BJ purposefully, then started looking in the cupboard under the stairs for his gardening gloves.

"I say," said BJ brightly, "what shall I do?"

"You?" snorted Dad. "I'll tell you what you can do."

He bent down and wagged his finger in BJ's face. "Nothing," he said. "Absolutely nothing. You just sit there, and don't do a thing. Do you hear me? You've caused enough trouble already this morning."

BJ gulped. "Oh. So you don't want me to clear up all this mess on the carpet then?"

Dad snorted. "You, clear up? You're a dog, dogs don't clear up messes. They make them!"

With that, he sneezed loudly, and walked off towards the back door. "And they smell," he muttered.

"Johnny," whispered BJ sadly.

"Yes?"

"I don't think your father likes me. I'd better not stay – I'll only get you in trouble."

Johnny looked out of the window by the kitchen sink. He could see his father bending down planting daffodil bulbs, and he could hear him rumbling to himself under his breath.

"Don't worry about Dad, BJ. He's always a bit grumpy in the mornings. I'm sure he'd love you to stay. It's just that he's got quite a bit on his mind just now. Mum doesn't like the house to be messy when she comes home. And if she sees that lot in the hallway – she'll go crazy."

BJ wagged his tail. "Oh, goodie. You mean I can really stay here with you?"

Johnny nodded "I expect so."

"Yippee!" BJ leapt into the air, and gave a tiny woof. Then he smiled at Johnny, took out his monocle, cleaned it and put it back in again. "In that case, I'll just pop along and see if there's anything I can do to help. Pip, pip."

He trotted off into the hallway, and left Johnny alone with the washing up.

Shortly afterwards, Dad came back into the kitchen. "Right!" he said. "That's that little job taken care of. Now all we have to do is to clear up the carpet, and ..." He looked carefully all round the kitchen and lowered his voice. "Get rid of that stupid dog."

"Dad! How can you say that about BJ? He isn't stupid. He can talk for goodness sake."

"So what? He's still nothing but a nuisance. All dogs are."

"He found the back door keys you lost, Dad."

"And he dug up half the garden."

Johnny sighed.

"Anyway," said Dad. "I haven't got time to stand around here chatting all day. Your mother is due home in five minutes, and I've still got to clear up that carpet." He disappeared off into the hallway.

Seconds later, he was back again. "I can't believe it." He looked dumbstruck.

"Can't believe what?" asked Johnny, drying his hands.

"It's gone."

"What has?"

"All that mess. It's gone," repeated Dad.

Johnny frowned. "But how? Who can possibly have cleaned it up?"

He looked at his father, and then gulped. "Are you thinking what I'm thinking, Dad?"

His father nodded. Johnny smiled.

"BJ," they said together.

At that moment, the front doorbell rang.

"Quick, Johnny," hissed Dad. "It's your mother. Now remember – don't tell her anything about the mess on her new carpet. All right? It would send her crazy. Talking of which ..."

He frowned. "Where's BJ? We mustn't let her see him. If she finds out that we've got a dog in the house – she'll go crackers. You know what she thinks of dogs – she hates them even more than I do. Who knows what she'll think if she finds out you've discovered a dog that can talk!"

Johnny gulped. His father was right. About the only thing his Mum disapproved of, more than she disapproved of messiness – was dogs.

It was essential that they kept BJ out of sight.

"You're right, Dad," hissed Johnny. "We've got to find BJ before Mum does. She always said that the only animal she was ever going to allow in this house was you!"

Dad nodded. "I know. Let's go."

They ran into the hallway and were just in time to see BJ opening the front door.

"No," they yelled. But it was too late.

"Hello," said BJ politely to Mum, as she stood waiting on the doorstep. "You must be Mum. My name's BJ – and I must say, I'm glad you didn't get here any earlier."

"Why?" asked Mum. BJ wagged his tail happily.

"Because the whole house was in a frightful mess ... especially your new carpet!"

"Oh, no," groaned Dad and Johnny together. "Now what?"

Chapter 2
Dad gets into Trouble

Mrs Buckett – otherwise known as Johnny's mum stepped silently, into the hallway. She put down the suitcase she was carrying, looked at BJ and then frowned at her husband, Henry. Otherwise known as Johnny's dad.

"Hello, darling," he said nervously. "You're just in time for dinner. How was Auntie Mary?" There was no reply.

He tried again.

"We've had a lovely time, haven't we, Johnny?"
He looked across at Johnny hopefully.

Johnny nodded, and tried to think of something to say. He was worried – his Mum was never quiet!

At this point, BJ wagged his tail, and looked as if he

was about to speak. He wanted to tell Mum what a lovely time they had been having – cleaning carpets, and re-burying daffodil bulbs!

But before he could say a word, Johnny bent down and covered his mouth with a firm hand. "Be quiet," he hissed. "You've said more than enough already!"

He looked up at his Mum and smiled. It wasn't a very convincing smile, but it was the best he could manage under the circumstances.

"Hello, Mum. Did you have a nice trip?" he said brightly.

Still without saying a word, his mother took off her gloves and placed them on the shelf above the radiator.

She looked very thoughtful.

Johnny's father gulped. He didn't like it when his wife was quiet. It was a bad sign. It usually meant that somebody was in trouble. And usually, that somebody was him!

He looked at his wife, and then at BJ. "Come on, Johnny," he hissed. "Hurry up and take that stupid animal outside before he gets me in any more trouble."

He turned and smiled at Mum. "I'm afraid Johnny has been trying to persuade me to let him keep a pet in the house." He gave a false laugh. "Of course, I told him that he couldn't – you don't approve of pets. Do you dear?" he said hopefully.

There was no answer.

Dad patted Johnny on the head. "You see? I told you that your Mum would never let you keep a dog in the house." He sighed with relief – he had decided that BJ was bad news and that the sooner he disappeared, the happier Dad would be.

"So you just take the dog outside, Johnny, and let him go. I think that's the best thing to do, isn't it dear?"

He smiled at his wife, and waited for her to agree with him. But she didn't. Instead, she removed her coat and hung it on the rack behind the front door. Then, still in silence, she frowned at herself in the hallway mirror.

"Right," she said. "First things first!" She pinched herself on the forearm. "Ouch!"

"What are you doing, Mum?" asked Johnny.

"Just making sure that I'm not dreaming – it's not every day you find your front door being opened by a talking dog."

Johnny opened his eyes wide, and tried to look innocent. "What do you mean? A talking dog?"

His mother sighed. "I'm very pleased to see that you are a terrible liar, Johnny Buckett. It proves that you haven't had much practice!" She looked at Dad. "Unlike your father!"

"Me!" gasped Dad. "What have I done wrong?"

Mum looked at him. "I don't know … yet. But you're bound to have done something. You always do when I leave you in charge!"

BJ nodded. "She's right, Dad. You did leave your bike in the hallway, after all."

Johnny groaned. "BJ! I told you to keep quiet!"

But it was too late. Mum had already heard him.

"So that's why my new carpet was so filthy! No doubt you took your new bicycle out in all that rain last night – didn't you?"

Dad hung his head. "Yes, dear."

"Then left it in my nice, clean hallway – to drip all over the carpet."

Dad sneezed.

"And now you've caught a cold," continued Mum. "Well, it's your own fault."

Johnny's father gulped. It was time to make a sharp exit, before she gave him a lecture.

"I'll just take your suitcase upstairs for you," he said quickly. "Then I'll cook you your dinner – you must be starving. All right?"

Before Mum could answer, he snatched up the suitcase and shot up the stairs.

"Phew," he muttered, as he crept into his bedroom and closed the door behind him. "What a narrow escape!" He lay down on the bed, took off his glasses, and sneezed.

"It's not fair, this shouldn't be happening to me – I'm really ill! It's all BJ's fault. The last thing I need is a talking dog in the house, getting me into trouble whenever he opens his mouth!" He closed his eyes. "And the first thing I need is a nice, long snooze."

He turned over, and was soon fast asleep.

Meanwhile, downstairs, Mum was sitting on the sofa in the living room, with Johnny sitting next to her.

BJ was on her lap. Strangely enough, she appeared to be in quite a good mood!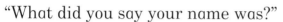

She tickled BJ behind the ears and smiled, gently.

"What did you say your name was?"

BJ wagged his tail. He liked being tickled behind the ears.

"Hmm?" he said. "What was that?"

"He's called BJ," said Johnny.

Mum nodded. "Oh, yes. I remember." She grinned. "I don't normally like dogs, BJ. But I must say – I don't think you're a normal dog!" She stopped herself. "You are a dog, aren't you?"

"Sort of." BJ took out his monocle and cleaned it. He looked as if he was trying very hard to be modest. He gave in, and sighed.

"Actually, you're right – I'm not a normal dog at all!"

"I thought not," said Mum. "Tell me, why can you talk?"

Johnny nodded. "That's a good question, Mum. Why can you talk, BJ? I've never heard of a talking dog before."

BJ stared at him through his monocle. "Really?"

"Honestly."

"Good grief," muttered BJ. "All the dogs talk where I come from."

"Where do you come from?" asked Mum.

"The Planet Z," replied BJ. "It's next to The Planet Y."

"So what are you doing on Earth?" asked Johnny.

BJ grinned. "Homework, actually!"

"Huh?"

BJ nodded and sat up on Mum's lap. "I'm doing a project called 'People Who Live on Earth'. So I've come here to do some research. The thing is ..." He looked around the room suspiciously. "I'm not supposed to tell anyone," he lowered his voice, "because it's a secret. No one must ever find out that I'm from another planet, or else I'll get in lots of trouble from my teacher. She says that it would affect my results, and ruin my project." He winked cheerfully at Johnny.

"Oh dear," said Mum.

"What's wrong?" asked BJ.

"Well, we know that you come from another planet. You've just told us!"

For the second time that day, BJ looked very sad.

His tail drooped, his face fell, and even his monocle seemed to lose its sparkle. "You're right," he said. "That's torn it."

"Never mind," said Mum. "We won't tell anybody – will we, Johnny?"

Johnny shook his head. "Of course not."

"But you don't understand. My teacher will be very annoyed with me. She said that I mustn't let anyone know – or else it would ruin my project. She said that people would start acting strangely when they found out I could talk." BJ looked thoroughly dejected. "Me and my big mouth."

He looked up at Johnny. "It was just that you seemed so nice and friendly. I had to say hello, and now I've ruined everything." He gulped and, for a moment, it looked as if he was about to cry.

Mum stroked his head.

"There, there, BJ. Don't you worry. I'm sure we'll think of something," she said gently.

She was quiet for a minute, then she snapped her fingers. "I know what to do. I'll write a letter to your teacher, explaining that you didn't mean to tell us where you came from. That it was an accident."

BJ immediately cheered up. "I say. Would you?" he asked. "That would be ever so kind."

Mum nodded. "Of course I would. That way your teacher won't be at all annoyed with you. And as for ruining the results of your project, we'll just carry on as usual – we won't start acting strangely. Will we, Johnny?"

"No, we won't change a bit," replied Johnny. "Honestly."

"Yippee!" cried BJ. He jumped into the air and gave a little woof.

Johnny smiled.

Mum laughed. "There again, having said that, your father always acts pretty strange – even at the best of times." She looked at her watch.

"Talking of your father, where has he got to? He's supposed to be cooking the dinner. I'm starving."

"Don't worry," said Johnny. "I'll go and find him."

Five minutes later, Johnny walked into his father's bedroom and sat on the bed.

"Dad," he said softly, "are you awake?"

There was no reply, except for a long drawn out snore.

"I suppose that means no," thought Johnny.

He shook his father gently by the shoulder. "Dad. Wake up!"

His father rolled over and groaned. "Leave me alone, I'm really ill!"

"No you aren't, you've just got a cold."

"That's what I said – I'm in a serious state. Now leave me alone – I'm not getting up."

Johnny sighed. There was only one way to deal with his father when he was in this sort of mood.

You had to frighten him.

"You certainly will be in a serious state, if you don't hurry up and cook the dinner like you promised you would. Mum's really hungry. She says that if you haven't got everything ready in twenty minutes – you're for the high jump!"

Dad leapt up from his bed and shoved his glasses on to the end of his nose. "What did you say?"

Johnny smiled. That trick worked every time. "I said that you've got twenty minutes to cook the dinner."

Dad looked around the room nervously. "Where's your mother?"

"In the bath."

Dad nodded. "Good. Where's that troublesome dog?"

"Outside."

Dad rubbed his hands together, happily. "Good riddance. You mark my words, Johnny. Dogs are nothing but a nuisance – we'll be better off without him."

Johnny thought for a moment. Then he decided not to tell his Dad that BJ had only gone outside to get some fresh air. He was bound to find out for himself, sooner or later.

Dad stood up and smiled. "Come on, Johnny. Let's go down to the kitchen." He grinned. "I shall take something out of the fridge and heat it up. Then we can all celebrate getting rid of that stupid, smelly dog." He began to sing to himself.

"Am I still in trouble with your mother about the carpet?" he asked.

Johnny shrugged. "I don't really know."

Dad winked at him. "I'm sure she'll forgive me after I've cooked her a lovely meal. Come on." He opened the bedroom door. "I'll race you down to the kitchen!"

Two minutes and thirty-five seconds later, Dad closed the fridge and groaned. "Oh no!"

"What's wrong, Dad?" asked Johnny.

By way of an answer, his father pointed to the long shopping list stuck to the door of the fridge by a magnetic sheep. "I forgot to go shopping yesterday. There's absolutely nothing in the house to eat – except for a few tins and things."

He sighed. "It's no use, I've got to go and get something from the shops." He looked at his watch. "Which means that I won't have dinner ready in twenty minutes – Mum will be furious with me."

"Is there anything I can do?" asked Johnny.

"Yes," said Dad. "Could you lay the table?"

Johnny nodded.

"Oh, and, Johnny, don't tell your mother that I forgot to go shopping yesterday. It'll just get me in even more trouble. Just tell her that I've had to pop out to get some more milk, or something, all right?"

Johnny nodded, again. He would think of something to say to Mum that wasn't a lie. She was right, he was a terrible liar. Thankfully.

"Bye," said Dad. He ran down the hallway and out of the front door.

At that moment, the back door opened and BJ

strolled in. "I say," he said. "Where's Dad off to in such a hurry?"

Johnny explained about the forgotten shopping trip.

BJ frowned. "But today's Sunday, isn't it?"

"Yes."

"I thought all the shops closed on a Sunday."

Johnny gasped. "You're right, they do. That means Dad won't be able to get any food. He really will be in trouble with Mum."

BJ waved a paw airily. "Not at all. I'll cook the dinner – I love cooking." he opened the cupboard under the sink and examined the saucepans inside. He looked thoughtfully at Johnny.

"You'll have to help me though, I'm afraid this kitchen wasn't made for a dog to use. Everything is the wrong size!"

Fifteen minutes later, Mum walked into the breakfast room and sat down at the table. She sniffed the air. "Mmm. Smells lovely!"

The kitchen door opened, and Johnny poked his head round. "Hello, Mum. Dinner's almost ready."

"What is it?"

Johnny shrugged. "I don't really know. You'll have to ask the cook."

"Well, you can tell your father that it smells delicious. If it tastes as good as it smells, I shall forget all about my carpet getting dirty."

Just then, the front door opened and Dad walked in clutching a small plastic bag. He looked very worried. Nearly all the shops had been shut. The only thing he had managed to buy was a cheese and onion sandwich.

Mum smiled at him. "I was just telling Johnny how lovely the dinner smells."

"Pardon?" Dad frowned, and looked down at the plastic bag containing the cheese and onion sandwich. He sniffed it. "I can't smell anything."

Mum burst out laughing. "You are so silly sometimes, Henry. Come and sit down."

Still looking puzzled, Dad sat down at the table. The kitchen door opened again – and Johnny appeared carrying a huge bowl of steaming pasta. He put it down on the table and went out again.

"You are thoughtful, Henry," said Mum. "You know I love pasta."

At that moment, Johnny reappeared, holding a

steaming saucepan. He put it down on the table, and shot back into the kitchen.

Mum breathed in some of the steam. "Beautiful," she sighed. "What is it?"

Dad gulped. "I don't know."

"What do you mean – you don't know?" asked Mum with a smile.

"I mean – it's a surprise," replied Dad, looking very surprised. He stood up. "Excuse me, I just want to go and make sure everything's all right."

He ran into the kitchen, taking his plastic bag with him.

"Johnny," he hissed. "You're a genius – I didn't know that you could cook. You've saved my life!" He threw the plastic bag into the bin with a smile on his face.

"Oh, it wasn't me," said Johnny, putting some dishes into the dishwasher. "It was him," he pointed.

"Oh, no!" groaned Dad. "I don't believe it."

There, standing on a stool next to the cooker, was BJ – wagging his tail and wearing a chef's hat.

Dad gulped. "Your mother can't eat something cooked by a dog – it's bound to taste disgusting!"

He ran back into the breakfast room just in time to see Mum swallowing her first mouthful of Pasta Surprise.

"Now what do I do?" he cried.

Shortly afterwards, Mum put down her fork and pushed away her empty plate. "That was the best pasta I have ever tasted in my entire life," she sighed.

"Well done, Henry," she smiled across at her husband.

"Do you know what? I never realised that you were such a good cook. Normally, you just take something out of the freezer and heat it up – and it tastes horrible."

Dad frowned. "Does it?"

Mum nodded. "But that pasta was fantastic!" She laughed. "And to think, I honestly thought that you would forget to go shopping." She shook her head. "It just shows how wrong I was to doubt you."

Dad looked hurt. "You didn't really think that I would forget to go shopping. Did you?"

"I did – and I was wrong. You must have spent hours planning that meal, buying the stuff in, and then cooking it."

"Well," said Dad, trying to sound modest – and failing. "I do my best." He smiled weakly at Mum.

"I am such a lucky woman to have a husband like you."

"You are?" said Dad, slightly amazed.

"Yes, I am. And I'll never tell you off for bringing your bike into the house, ever again."

Dad grinned, he could hardly believe his luck!

Perhaps BJ wasn't such a bad dog to have around the house, after all. He couldn't remember the last time his wife had been so nice to him.

He closed his eyes and leant back in his chair – totally happy.

At that moment, the kitchen door opened and Johnny appeared carrying two bowls of ice cream. He was followed by BJ, still wearing the chef's hat.

"Did you enjoy the pasta?" asked BJ.

Mum nodded.

"I'm glad," replied BJ. "I would have cooked something a little more exciting ... only Dad forgot to go shopping." He smiled.

Mum frowned. "So you cooked the pasta."

BJ nodded.

"And did Dad forget to go shopping?"

BJ nodded again.

"Hen-ry," growled Mum. "I want a word with you!"

But Dad was nowhere to be seen. He was hiding underneath the table.

"Why does that dog always say the wrong thing at the wrong time?" he groaned.

Chapter 3
BJ Stays

Later on that day, just as Johnny was about to go into his Mum and Dad's bedroom, he heard a strange noise.

"Psst!"

He looked down at his feet to see if he had trodden on anything. But he hadn't. He frowned, and then looked slightly worried.

It had suddenly dawned on him where he had heard that strange noise before.

He shook his head. "Impossible. Dad would never do a thing like that – he's not that stupid." It sounded for all the world as if his father had brought his bike back into the house – only this time there was a puncture in one of the tyres.

"Psst!" It was the strange noise again. Johnny

looked all around the landing and down the stairs – there was no one to be seen anywhere. He scratched his head thoughtfully.

He was sure that he hadn't imagined it.

He stood still, very quietly, and waited for the noise to start up again. But it didn't.

"How very mysterious," he muttered, feeling very mystified. He shrugged his shoulders. "Still, I haven't got time to stand around all day. I've got to find Dad."

He put his hand on the doorknob of his parents' room and was just about to push open the door, when he heard a creaking noise from the other side of the landing. He looked, and was just in time to see the door to his own bedroom open slightly.

He frowned. "That's not just mysterious. That's weird."

Seconds later, a hand came out, and a finger beckoned him inside. "Psst!"

Johnny sighed.

"Dad! It was you – you had me worried there for a minute. I thought I was hearing things!"

His father's head appeared. "Sssh," he put his finger to his lips. "Keep your voice down," he whispered, "or else you won't be the only one who's hearing things." He opened the door wide and beckoned Johnny inside. "Come in, quick!"

Johnny stepped silently into his bedroom with a puzzled look on his face. "What do you mean? I won't be the only one who is hearing things?" he whispered.

His father looked all round the landing, then ever so gently, closed the door with a soft click. He turned and faced his son. "I mean, that I don't want your mother to hear you talking to me," he hissed. "I'm in her bad books at the moment."

"I wouldn't say that exactly," said Johnny.

"Well, I would."

Johnny ignored him, and looked curiously all round the room. A thought had occurred to him. "Hey, what are you doing in my bedroom anyway, Dad?"

His father didn't answer.

Suddenly Johnny smiled. "I know. You're hiding from Mum, aren't you?"

His father tried to look innocent and hurt – as if the very idea of hiding from his wife had never occurred to him.

He failed.

Johnny grinned. "It's no use trying to deny it, Dad. I know that you're hiding from Mum."

"How?"

"It's obvious. Look," Johnny pointed. The door to his wardrobe was wide open. It looked as if someone had been sitting on the pile of clean clothes inside. They were all squashed and creased.

"You always hide in my wardrobe when you don't want Mum to find you!"

Dad tried to look innocent – but failed, again.

Johnny shook his head. "It's ridiculous, Dad. You act more like a kid than I do. You are going to have to grow up, one day."

"Nonsense! I am grown up, thank you very much," said his father crossly.

"No you're not," replied Johnny. "Grown ups don't hide in wardrobes."

His father opened his mouth to speak – and then closed it again. He had just realised that Johnny was right. He tried to think of a good excuse for his behaviour.

But he couldn't.

"Anyway," continued Johnny, after a few seconds of silence, "I'm not going to argue. What did you want me for?"

Dad put his hands in his pockets, shrugged, and
looked down at his feet. He began to move them in
circles on the carpet, as if he was slightly
embarrassed.

"What do I want you for? Oh, nothing much. It's just that I was bored. And I couldn't find your remote control car."

Johnny looked puzzled. "Why on earth were you looking for my remote control car?"

"I wanted to play with it," muttered Dad.

Johnny burst out laughing. "See what I mean? Most grown ups don't play with remote control cars, either." He shook his head, and tutted to himself.

Suddenly he stopped, and looked serious. "Hey, I've just remembered why I came upstairs. Mum's in the living room and she wants to see you."

Dad looked nervous. "What for?"

"I don't know – exactly." Johnny went over to his wardrobe and began to rearrange the clothes that had been sat upon.

His father started to panic.

"I bet it's that stupid dog. He's probably said something to her – and got me in even more trouble." He rubbed the side of his face, the way he always did when he was getting worried. "I wonder what it is this time?"

He took out his handkerchief and blew his nose. "It's not fair – I'm really ill! That BJ has already got me in enough hot water today. First, he went and told Mum about me getting the carpet dirty. And then, he went and told her that I'd forgotten to go shopping. Now what has he said?"

He scowled. "If there's one thing I hate more than dogs – it's talking dogs. The sooner we get rid of him, the better."

Johnny put down a shirt he was holding and thought for a minute. "Actually, now I think about it, Dad, I don't think you are in trouble. Mum just said something about your clothes."

It was Dad's turn to look puzzled. "What about my clothes?"

Johnny shrugged. "I don't know. I think she wants to know what clothes you're going to be wearing tonight."

"Why?" asked Dad.

Johnny finished folding up his clothes and closed the wardrobe door. "I haven't got a clue." He turned to face his father. "What's wrong, Dad?"

His father had suddenly gone very pale.

"You're not going to faint again, are you?" said Johnny.

"It doesn't suit you!"

His father shook his head slowly, and then sat on the edge of the bed. He looked dazed. "So that's why Mum's in such a mood with me." He smacked his hand against his forehead. "I'd forgotten all about it."

"Forgotten all about what?" asked Johnny.

"About tonight!"

"What about tonight?"

Dad groaned. "It's our wedding anniversary ... and I'm taking Mum to the cinema." He gave a low moan, and began to rock from side to side with his head in his hands. He sounded heartbroken.

"What's so bad about that?" asked Johnny. "Mum doesn't know that you've forgotten about your wedding anniversary."

His father ignored him.

"Cheer up, Dad," said Johnny sitting down beside him on the bed. "It's going to be all right."

His father smiled weakly, and shook his head again. He patted Johnny's knee. "You don't understand, Johnny. It isn't going to be all right. Mum's bound to find out that I've forgotten all about our wedding anniversary."

"How? I won't tell her."

Dad sighed. "You won't need to. I promised to give her a diamond ring as a present."

Johnny grinned. "Oh, yes. I remember her telling me about it. She sounded really excited. I think that was a great idea of yours, Dad."

"Except for one thing. I told her that she could have it tonight ..."

Johnny shrugged. "So what's the problem?"

For several seconds, his father looked at him in silence. Johnny closed his eyes and gulped. He had suddenly realised what had happened.

"No," he said, "you didn't?"

His father gulped. "Yes, I did."

Johnny sat down on the bed next to his father, and put his head in his hands. "Don't tell me," he groaned. "You forgot to buy the ring!"

Dad nodded.

"Mum is going to be furious," whispered Johnny.

At that moment, the bedroom door opened, and BJ bounded in. He looked very pleased about something. "I say," he said, quivering with excitement. "I've got some wonderful news for you." He peered at them both through his monocle. "Can you guess what it is?"

Dad looked up. For a brief second he almost managed to look cheerful. "Don't tell me – you're leaving!" he said hopefully.

"No," BJ shook his head. "I'm staying. Isn't it super?" He dashed once round the room, and then leapt on to the bed, landing on Johnny's lap. "Mum says it's all right."

Johnny lifted his head and grunted. He hadn't really been listening to what BJ had said. He was too busy trying to think of a way to help his father.

"Great news, isn't it?" BJ rolled over on to his back, and started kicking his legs in the air.

Johnny tickled him behind the ears gently. "If you say so, BJ." He was still thinking about poor Dad. He was going to be in real trouble when Mum realised that he had forgotten to get her ring.

"Yippee," squealed BJ. "I'm so excited – I want to sing." He began barking loudly.

Dad groaned. "That's the worst singing I've ever heard."

BJ stopped and sat up.
"I know, I'm a terrible singer. It's just that I'm so excited about staying with you all." He began to bark once more.

Dad groaned again. "You what? You're going to stay!" He put his head back in his hands and covered his ears. "That's the worst news I've ever heard."

BJ, who was far too busy barking to hear what Dad was saying, wagged his tail. He smiled at Johnny, and took a deep breath. "It was Mum's idea. She says I can stay as long as I like – until I've finished all my homework. Isn't it marvellous? Hmm?"

There was something about him that was so cheerful and so happy, that it made Johnny realise that something was going on. But he wasn't exactly sure what it was. He blinked. "What did you say, BJ? Did Mum say that you can stay?

BJ nodded.

Johnny smiled, and thought about it for a second. After a while, he found himself forgetting all about Dad's problems and Mum's ring. Instead of looking worried, he found himself grinning from ear to ear.

BJ's words had finally sunk in.

"You're staying?"

BJ nodded. "Isn't it super?"

Johnny jumped up. "Yes, it is," he cried, forgetting all about his Dad and his worries. "It's totally brilliant!"

He threw the little dog into the air. Then caught
him again, and began dancing round in circles.

Dad snorted. "Well personally, I think it's terrible."
He stood up. "I've got enough problems as it is. The
last thing I need is a stupid dog around the house,

making a mess and dropping hairs all over the place."

He scowled at BJ. But BJ was so busy being excited that he hadn't heard a word that Dad had said.

Dad sneezed. "But who cares about me – or what I think? No one, that's who." He stomped across the room, still muttering to himself, and yanked open the bedroom door.

He turned and took one last look at BJ. "Dogs!" he muttered. "Who needs them? Not me – that's for sure."

Then he went down the stairs to find Mum.

"BJ," said Johnny, a few minutes later when they had both calmed down, "we've got to do something about Dad."

BJ was lying on the floor at the time, trying to get his breath back. He looked up at Johnny through his monocle and frowned. "What do you mean – do something about Dad?"

Johnny sighed. "He's in trouble with Mum."

"You know what?" said BJ thoughtfully. "Your Dad always seems to be in trouble with Mum."

"Oh, he isn't usually. It's just that you keep on opening your mouth and landing him in it."

BJ looked surprised. "Do I?"

"Yes." Johnny scratched his ear. "But it isn't your fault this time." He explained all about the diamond ring that his father had forgotten to get.

When he had finished, BJ looked very thoughtful. He was silent for a long time. Then he nodded slowly, as if he had just realised something.

"That explains it."

"Explains what?" asked Johnny.

"Why Dad wasn't very excited about me staying."

"Oh no," said Johnny, without thinking. "That's because he thinks you're a pain."

"What?" BJ's face fell.

Johnny realised his mistake. BJ was very sensitive about some things, and people thinking that he was 'a pain', was obviously one of them.

"What I mean is," said Johnny quickly. "Dad thinks all dogs are a pain. Not just you."

But it was too late, BJ wasn't listening, his ears had sagged, his tail had drooped and his monocle had lost its sparkle. He gulped. "It's all right. I won't stay if I'm not wanted." His bottom lip began to quiver and it looked as if he was about to cry.

"It's not that Dad doesn't want you to stay," said
Johnny quickly. He licked his lips and wondered what
to say next. The trouble was, he knew perfectly well
that BJ was right. Dad didn't want him to stay.

"What is it then?" asked BJ, sadly.

Johnny shrugged his shoulders. "It's just that you
keep on getting him into trouble with Mum –
that's all."

"I don't mean to."

"I know you don't," said Johnny, as softly as he
could. "I'm sure that if you could only think of a way
to help Dad for once, he'd love you to stay." He crossed
his fingers behind his back, so BJ couldn't see them.
"At least, I hope he would," he whispered quietly.

"But how could I help him?"

Johnny decided it was time to try and cheer BJ up. He smiled. "Well, you could always find him a diamond ring to give to Mum, I suppose." He burst out laughing.

"Could I?" asked BJ hopefully. Johnny picked him up. "I was only joking, BJ. Diamond rings are really expensive, you could never afford to buy one. And ..." he patted BJ's head, "it's Sunday, remember, all the shops are shut."

BJ looked up. "Oh, I wouldn't buy it. I'd make it."

Johnny burst out laughing again. "Don't be ridiculous. You can't make a diamond ring, just like that."

BJ raised an eyebrow.

Johnny stopped laughing and frowned. There was

something about BJ's face that made Johnny think he wasn't joking.

"You couldn't really make a diamond ring ... could you?" he asked, in amazement.

BJ winked. "You can do anything – if you try hard enough. Anyway," he jumped down to the floor and shook himself, "I've got work to do. Pip, pip."

With that, he strolled out of the bedroom, and disappeared from sight.

Five minutes later, Dad was sitting in his bedroom on the edge of his bed with his head in his hands. He was also wearing his best suit and his favourite brown tie. He groaned. "What am I going to do?"

Just then, the door opened and BJ walked in. He looked as if he had been very busy. "I've got something for you," said BJ, quietly. He placed a small, black box in front of Dad, and stepped back.

He sniffed, as if he was upset about something.

Dad looked at BJ, and then at the box. "What's inside it?" he asked gruffly. He sounded as if he didn't really care – which he didn't. BJ shrugged. "Nothing much. Just something I made for you."

"What is it?" Dad still didn't sound at all interested.

"A going-away present."

Dad snorted. "But I'm not going anywhere."

"Not you. Me. I'm going away," BJ gulped, as if he was finding it hard to speak. "If you don't want me to stay – I won't." He turned away. "I know you don't like me," he said sadly.

Dad looked a bit embarrassed. He picked up the box, and examined it. He didn't know what to say. "So why have you given me a going-away present then?" he asked, after a while.

"Because I like you. And I want you to know that I didn't mean to get you in trouble with Mum."

BJ wiped his eye, and began to snuffle. "And ... and," he gulped, "I hope that this little present will get you out of trouble. That's all."

Dad snorted. "The only thing that would get me out of trouble just now, is a diamond ring."

BJ didn't reply. Instead he nodded sadly to himself and walked slowly to the door. He turned to face Dad.

"There's only one thing I would like to say before I go, Dad."

"What?" mumbled Dad. For some reason he felt uncomfortable. He should have been really happy that BJ was going, but instead, he felt a bit guilty.

He opened the small, black box.

Inside it, was a beautiful diamond ring.

Perhaps he had been a bit too harsh on BJ – all things considered.

"What is it, BJ?" he said.

BJ blinked at him through his monocle and sniffed back another tear. "That's the wrong tie to wear with that suit. It would look a lot better if you wore your green stripy one." And with that, he was gone.

Dad watched him go, and felt a lump come to his throat. "This is ridiculous," muttered Dad. "I should be glad to see the back of that troublesome dog."

Half an hour later, Johnny ran into the living room. His mother and father were standing in front of the fire, holding hands. His father had on his best suit ... and a green, stripy tie.

"Look what your father has just given me, Johnny," said Mum. She showed him her hand. On one of her fingers was a beautiful diamond ring.

Johnny gasped and looked at Dad. "But how on earth ..." he stopped himself.

Dad laughed. "It's all right, Johnny. Mum knows all about it. I've told her how I forgot to go and get her the ring I promised – and how BJ very kindly made this one for me so that I wouldn't get into trouble."

Mum nodded. "It's true. I know everything."

Johnny gulped. "Not everything, Mum." He blinked. "I can't find BJ anywhere. I think he's gone. He said that he wasn't going to stay if he wasn't wanted – and now he's gone."

Dad burst out laughing.

"It's not funny, Dad," cried Johnny, angrily. "It's all your fault he's gone in the first place. He thinks you don't like him – because he keeps on getting you into trouble!"

Dad shook his head. "He doesn't think that at all," he said with a smile. "Not now. We've had a nice long chat, BJ and I have. And I've told him that he's welcome to stay for as long as he likes."

"Really?"

Dad nodded. "I realised that I had been too harsh on him. He means well – it's just that he often opens his mouth without thinking!"

"Then where is he?" cried Johnny, drying his eyes.

Mum smiled. "Having a little nap – he's dog tired."

Dad nodded. "And guess where he's sleeping?"

"I don't know," said Johnny. "All I know is – I can't find him anywhere."

Mum burst out laughing. "Where does Dad always go when he wants to have a bit of peace and quiet?"

Johnny looked at his father, and then at his mother. He frowned. "You don't mean ..."

His parents nodded.

"He's in your wardrobe," said Mum. "I told you that I know everything."